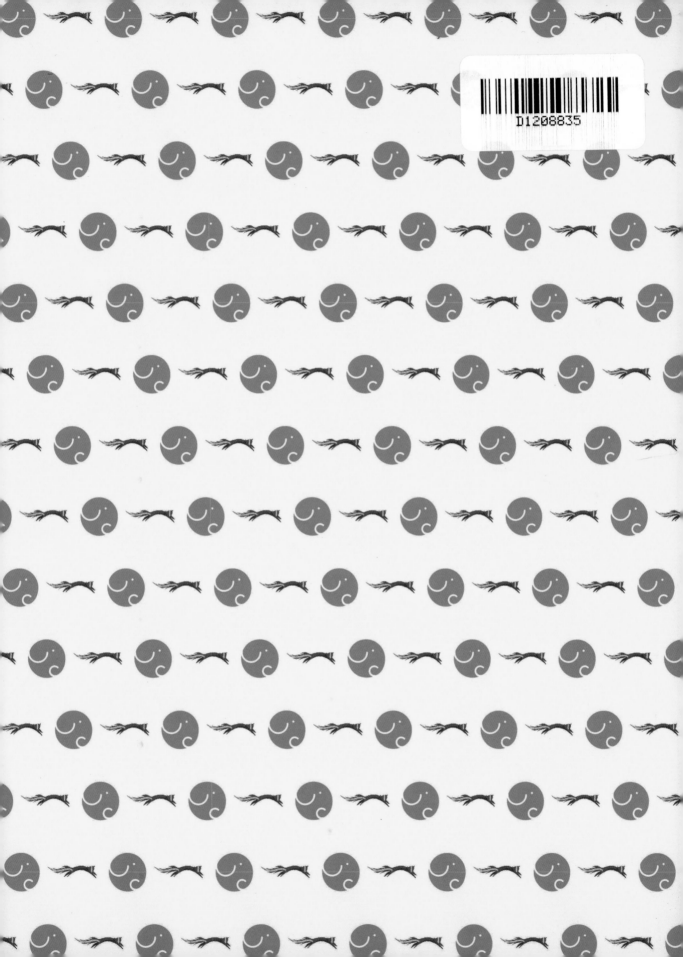

D1208835

To Neel, for his unending support; you are my rock and my best friend.
-Sailaja

For my parents, who inspired my love of words from the beginning.
-Amy

For Michael . . . for reminding me that I can move mountains.
-Tim

www.bharatbabies.com

Hanuman Moves a Mountain

©2017 Amy Maranville. All Rights Reserved. No part of this publication
may be reproduced, stored in a retrieval system or transmitted in any
form by any means electronic, mechanical, or photocopying, recording or
otherwise without the permission of the author.

For more information, please contact:
Mascot Books
560 Herndon Parkway #120
Herndon, VA 20170
info@mascotbooks.com
namaste@bharatbabies.com

Library of Congress Control Number: 2017908691

CPSIA Code: PRT0717A
ISBN-13: 978-1-63177-849-0

Printed in the United States

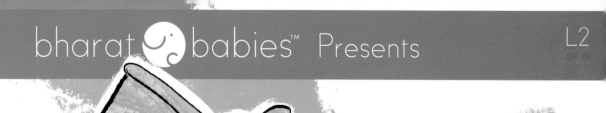

HANUMAN MOVES A MOUNTAIN

WORDS BY
AMY MARANVILLE

PICTURES BY
TIM PALIN

It had been a rainy morning. Harini stayed inside, building treehouses and pirate caves, waiting for the sun to come out.

But when the clouds cleared, Harini's Amma wouldn't let her go outside. "When you have finished playing, you should return your toys to their homes. Like Hanuman did with the mountain."

don't remember that story," said Harini.

will tell it to you while you clean," said Amma. "Do
ot worry—you will be outside before you know it."
nd so she began...

A long, long time ago, there was a great war. A powerful man named Ravana kidnapped the god Rama's wife, Seeta. He took her far away, to the land of Lanka.

Rama's brother Lakshmana, and his loyal friend Hanuman helped Rama to lead an army to Lanka. They wanted to bring Seeta home.

But Ravana's army was waiting for them.

Amidst the fighting, Ravana's son fired
a poisonous arrow high into the sky.

It flew through the air, and struck
Rama's brother Lakshmana in the heart.

The poison worked quickly, and Lakshmana fell into a deep sleep. Rama was very worried. Hanuman was worried too. He was loyal to Rama, and wanted to do everything he could to help.

So Hanuman brought Dhanvantari,
a wise doctor, to see Lakshmana.
"This man is very ill," said the doctor.

"The only cure for this poison is *sanjeevani*—a special herb. This herb grows only at night, and only on the highest mountain peak of the Himalayas."

Hanuman Dada laid his hand on Rama's shoulder. "I will go and get this herb," he said. "Do not worry."

And away he flew, far, far, far
over rivers and valleys, searching
for Mount Dronagari, where the
special plant grew.

When finally he found it, Hanuman Dada thought the mountain was the most lovely mountain he had ever seen.

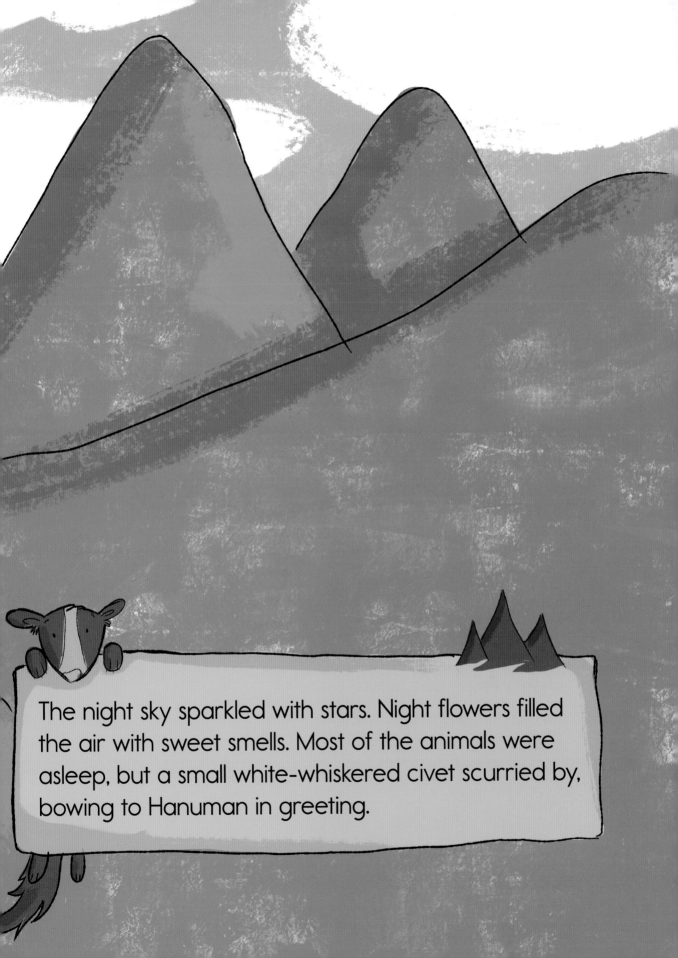

The night sky sparkled with stars. Night flowers filled the air with sweet smells. Most of the animals were asleep, but a small white-whiskered civet scurried by, bowing to Hanuman in greeting.

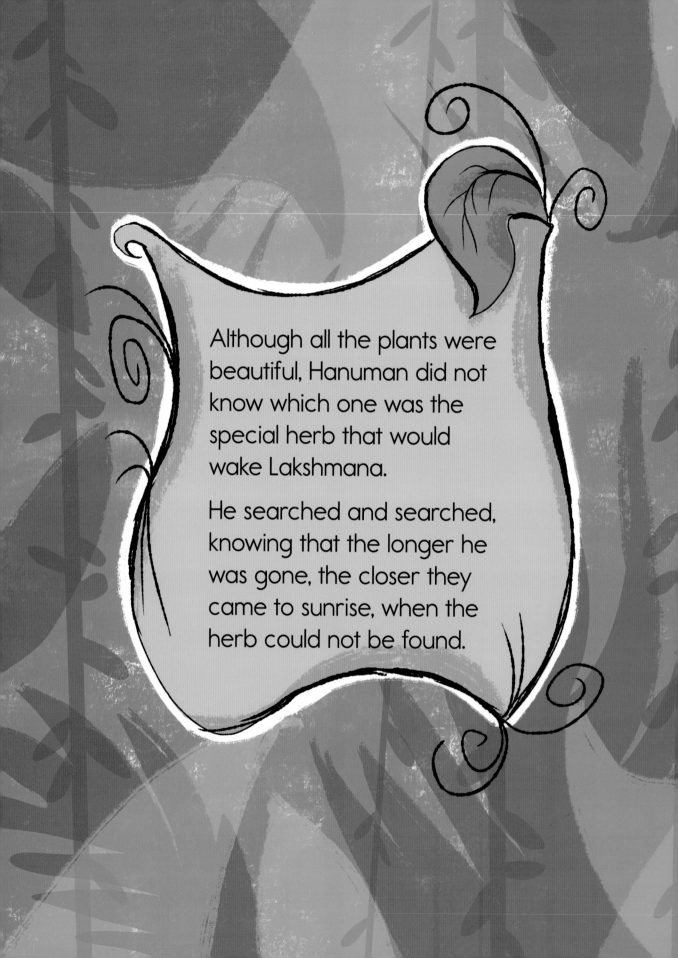

Although all the plants were beautiful, Hanuman did not know which one was the special herb that would wake Lakshmana.

He searched and searched, knowing that the longer he was gone, the closer they came to sunrise, when the herb could not be found.

At last, Hanuman knew he could look no longer. The dawn was coming soon, and there was no more time to search for the herb.

Using all his strength, Hanuman Dada reached to the bottom of the mountain and picked it up in his arms. The civet made a yowl of surprise as his home was lifted into the air.

Hanuman jumped into the air, carrying the mountain with him.

Flying faster than he ever had before, Hanuman Dada flew back over the rivers and valleys to Lanka, where his friend Lakshmana lay.

The doctor climbed onto the mountain, and selected just enough sanjeevani to heal Lakshmana.

He used the herb to brew a strong tea.

Gently, he helped Lakshmana sip the tea. All of a sudden, Lakshmana opened his eyes, and sat up.

Rama and Hanuman hugged Lakshmana with happiness.

With his friend feeling better, Hanuman Dada took a deep breath, lifted the mountain back onto his shoulders...

And carried the mountain back to its home.

"Because, you see, Hanuman had used the mountain for what he needed," Amma said. "And when he was finished, he returned it to its home."

"Just like my toys," said Harini.

"Yes, *kanna*. And look! They are all cleaned up. You can g[...] outside to play."

And Harini did.

Pronunciation Guide

Hi friends, you might notice that our pronunciation guide is a little different from other guides. We use familiar words to make pronunciations easier and more accessible. We hope this helps you learn more about the amazing cultures, religions, and people from South Asia.

Harini: haa-ri-nee

Amma: a-mm-aa
Another term for mother in many South Asian languages

Ravana: raa-va-naa
Evil king of Lanka

Hindu: hin-dh-oo
An individual who practices Hinduism

Rama: raa-maa
Hindu god and 7th incarnation of Lord Vishnu

Seeta: see-th-aa
Wife of Lord Rama

Lakshmana: luck-sh-maa-na
Brother of Lord Rama

Hanuman: ha-neu-maa-n
Son of the Wind God, Vayu, who takes the form of a monkey

Dhanavantari: dhaa-naa-vun-tha-ree
An ancient doctor

Sanjeevani: sun-jee-vaa-nee
Special herb with magic properties

Himalayas: him-aa-lay-aas
Tallest mountain range on Earth

Dada: daa-daa
Older brother

Dronagari: dh-roo-naa-gi-ree
Mountain in the Himalayas that has the special sanjeevani plant

Civet: si-ve-t
A small mammal native to the Himalayas

Kanna: kaa-n-aa
Term of endearment used by a parent to a child